# STEP BY STEP

# STEP BY STEP

Adapted by N.B. Grace

Based on the series created by Chris Thompson

Part One is based on the episode, "Shake It Up, Up, & Away: Part 1," written by Rob Lotterstein

Part Two is based on the episode, "Shake It Up, Up, & Away: Part 2," written by Eileen Conn

**DISNEP** PRESS

NEW YORK

# DANCE IT UP

Printed in the United States of America

First Edition

1 3 5 7 9 10 8 6 4 2

J689-1817-1-12350

ISBN 978-1-4231-6568-2

For more Disney Press fun, visit www.disneybooks.com
Visit DisneyChannel.com

**SUSTAINABLE FORESTRY INITIATIVE**

**Certified Chain of Custody**
Promoting Sustainable Forestry

www.sfiprogram.org
SFI-01054

The SFI label applies to the text stock

# STEP BY STEP

# CHAPTER 1

THE *SHAKE IT UP, CHICAGO* soundstage was buzzing as dancers got ready for the live show, which was just about to start. Performers dressed in black unitards with bits of yellow, red, purple, and green material on them were gathering near the stage. Others peered into makeup mirrors, checking their faces, which were painted with colorful stripes and zigzags. And everybody's heart was beating just a little bit faster as the beginning of the show got closer and closer.

At that moment, Gary Wilde, the show's host, raised his hand to get the dancers' attention.

"Everyone who's participating in the *Shake It Up Cares* trip to Alabama to clean up the wetlands, the bus leaves from here tomorrow morning at seven!" he announced.

CeCe Jones, one of the show's background dancers, tossed her hair to the side and sighed. Last month, it had seemed like a great idea to sign up for the trip. They would get to go on a road trip, help the environment, and maybe sign a few autographs for adoring fans. What could be better than that?

But now the reality was settling in—and it was not one that she liked.

"*Seven?*" she complained. "If *Shake It Up* really cared, they'd let us sleep in and pick us up at ten."

Her best friend, Rocky Blue, nodded in agreement. Rocky and CeCe both loved to dance, loved to perform, and loved to be onstage—what they definitely did *not* love was getting up early, even if it was for a good cause!

Gunther Hessenheffer, an exchange student from Germany and another background dancer on the show, saw this as his opportunity to make an impression on the show's host.

"Tinka and I will be there, Gary," he said eagerly, glancing at his twin sister.

Tinka grinned and nodded. After all, she and her brother were all about glamour and pizzazz—not to mention lots and lots of sequins. They had more style than any of the other dancers on *Shake It Up,* or so they thought. She could just imagine how stunned the local people would be when she and her brother crossed the state line into Alabama!

But Gary didn't respond. The *Shake It Up*

countdown clock had almost reached zero. They were about to go live!

"We're on in thirty seconds, people!" Gary shouted.

As the dancers scurried into position, Rocky smiled. How cool are we? she thought. Cleaning the environment, making a difference. She smiled brightly. After all, being a celebrity was great, but it was even better to use their fame to help other people.

At that moment, CeCe's phone chirped, signaling that she had a text message to read. As she glanced at the screen, her eyes widened with excitement.

"Ooh, breaking dance news!" she exclaimed. "They're holding open auditions this weekend for a new reality show called *Really? You Call That Dancing?*" She looked over at her best friend hopefully.

Rocky's face brightened at this news. "Hey,"

she said, "we should *totally* audition for that!"

In an instant, Rocky could see their future. She and CeCe would audition; they would be selected to compete; everyone in America would fall in love with them; they would win (of course); and, just like that, they would be superstars. It seemed so easy!

As if she knew exactly what Rocky was thinking, CeCe smiled back at her. "Yes! Thank you," she said with relief. "I am so happy I didn't have to trick or manipulate you into doing this. So, while our parents think we're in Alabama, we'll just sneak off to L.A."

Rocky's smile vanished. "It's in L.A.?" she asked, raising an eyebrow.

"Did I not mention that?" CeCe replied innocently.

Her friend gave her a warning look. "No!" Rocky yelled. "We are *not* sneaking off to L.A."

CeCe glared at Rocky, then blew a raspberry

in her direction. CeCe thought that sometimes, it was a real pain to have a friend whose first impulse was always to do the right thing!

Before they could argue about it, however, they heard Gary's voice floating down from his usual spot on the catwalk high above the stage.

"Welcome back to *Shake It Up, Chicago*, where we're about to *glow* your mind," he said.

Instantly, all the lights went out. Despite the darkness, the audience could still see all of the dancers, thanks to the pieces of colored material sewn to their costumes. Each dancer glowed in the dark!

CeCe, Rocky, and the other dancers started their routine. As the music thumped, the glowing slashes of red, purple, yellow, and green wiggled and bounced across the stage. The audience cheered and clapped along enthusiastically.

But even as CeCe went through the moves she had practiced so often, she was only thinking of one thing: How could she get Rocky to let go of her inhibitions and head with her to Los Angeles, where superstardom surely waited for them?

# CHAPTER 2

**CECE PUT ASIDE HER** scheming long enough to go to Crusty's, a pizza parlor owned by their friend Deuce Martinez's uncle. She and Rocky had been lucky enough to snag a table in the midst of a huge crowd that had gathered for the grand opening. They were sitting with Deuce, Rocky's brother Ty, and CeCe's little brother Flynn, sharing a pizza and waiting for the official opening ceremony to start.

They didn't have long to wait. Deuce's Uncle Frank, grinning, stepped out into the middle of the restaurant. Rocky thought she would have guessed that Deuce was his nephew even if she hadn't already known. Frank had the same dark hair, flashing white smile, and upbeat energy. As he got ready to address the crowd, two employees stood behind him holding up a large black cloth.

"Welcome to Crusty's, home of Chicago's deepest deep-dish pizza," Uncle Frank announced, waving to the crowd.

The crowd cheered appreciatively.

"And to prove it, we're going for a world record!" he added.

The two employees dropped the cloth, revealing a gigantic pizza! The crowd clapped and cheered even louder.

"I can't believe the best pizza in Chicago opened right on our block!" Rocky exclaimed.

"Yeah, with any luck, my mom will never cook again," CeCe said hopefully. Then she caught herself. "Oh! Who am I kidding?" She sighed. Her mother loved to cook, even though she wasn't very good at it.

"This pizza is great," Deuce said. "Well, you know, his secret is just–"

"Hey, hey, hey!" Uncle Frank interrupted. "Deuce, you weren't about to give away my secret ingredient, were you? This isn't your mom telling us all about your little battle with back acne. This is private."

Deuce winced. Why did relatives always have to mention embarrassing things in front of his friends?

"Everyone's met my Uncle Frank, right?" Deuce asked quickly.

The others nodded as Uncle Frank shook their hands and smiled. "Thanks so much for coming," he said.

"Good pizza," CeCe told him.

"Thank you," he replied. "Any friend of Deuce's gets a family discount, okay?"

Rocky and CeCe brightened. Since their salaries from *Shake It Up* were pretty small, they loved a good discount!

Then he added, "Zero percent off!"

Their faces fell. That was a pretty mean joke!

He chuckled. "I'm kidding–"

They looked happy again.

"–but I'm not." Still smiling, he hurried off to greet other customers.

CeCe took a thoughtful bite of pizza, which she was sorry to realize would never be discounted. She was still trying to think of some way to get Rocky to go along with her idea about ditching the charity work for stardom, but so far she hadn't come up with a plan that would work.

Before she could think of anything else, she was interrupted by her little brother, Flynn.

He heaved a deep sigh, looking glum.

"What's wrong, little man?" asked Ty.

"I'm in a rut," Flynn complained. "My life's a snooze. I go to school, come home, play, and then the cycle starts all over again. I feel like my best years are behind me."

Ty raised his eyebrows in surprise. "You're *eight*!" he protested. "It wasn't that long ago that you couldn't even talk."

"Yeah! The good old days," CeCe said under her breath.

Rocky stood up and put her hands on Flynn's shoulders. "You know what, Flynn?" she said as she leaned down and smiled with encouragement. "Life is what you make of it. So you need to go out there and find some excitement. Have an adventure!"

Flynn looked skeptical. "Easy for you to say," he replied. "*You're* allowed to cross the street by yourself."

Shaking his head, he wandered off into the crowd. Clearly, Rocky's little pep talk hadn't helped him—but it *had* given CeCe an idea.

CeCe took a deep breath and looked over at Rocky. "Dude," she said enthusiastically, "this is fun. It's just like being at a big Hollywood premiere party—"

"We're not going to L.A.," Rocky interrupted her. "We're going to *Alabama*."

"Come on, we should totally be auditioning for *Really? You Call That Dancing?*" CeCe pleaded, trying to sound convincing.

Rocky's dark brown hair swayed as she tilted her head to one side. "You know, I'd love to, but I'm already on a reality show called *My Best Friend Has Lost Her Mind*," she said sarcastically.

Before CeCe could respond, they were interrupted by Uncle Frank, who was yelling at one of his employees.

"All right, that's it!" Uncle Frank shouted at the

woman. "You're fired, you lazy, no-good bum!"

The woman gave him a disgusted look. Then she shook her head and stalked out of the pizza parlor.

Ty was watching the drama play out from his seat at the counter.

"Hey!" Ty called to Deuce, who was sitting at a nearby table. "Looks like there's an opening, and I'm saving up for a car," he said. "You're his nephew. Tell him to give me that job."

Ty grinned at Deuce confidently, already dreaming of the cool car he would buy with his earnings. Ty had no doubt that he would get the job. After all, how could Uncle Frank refuse a request from his own nephew? Not only that, but Ty was dressed with his usual professional polish. Even though he was just hanging out with friends, he had put on a lavender tie that went perfectly with his purple plaid shirt.

But Deuce just scoffed at Ty's hopes of

working for Uncle Frank. "I wouldn't count on that," he said. "That woman he just fired? His *mom*."

Ty's eyes widened in surprise.

Deuce walked over to the counter and sat on a stool next to Ty. "Besides, I've been thinking about hitting him up for a job myself," he revealed. He could always use extra cash!

Ty secretly thought that Deuce didn't have a chance. *Just look at the way he's dressed,* Ty thought. *A leather jacket and a garish T-shirt!* Deuce looked like a kid to Ty, not like someone responsible enough to get people their pizzas on time and piping hot.

But he wasn't going to tell his friend that, of course. No sense giving Deuce any ideas about sprucing up a bit!

Instead, Ty just shrugged.

"All right," he said. "Then fair's fair. Neither one of us will go for it."

"Okay," Deuce said, holding out his hand, and giving his friend a nod..

"Okay," Ty agreed, shaking on it.

Then they both slammed their hands down on the counter and, at the same time, shouted, "I want that job!"

# CHAPTER 3

**WHEN THE DAY FINALLY CAME** for the *Shake It Up, Chicago* cast to head off to Alabama, CeCe found, as usual, that she was running late. She had to be on the bus in less than an hour, and she still hadn't finished packing!

She hauled her suitcase into the living room of her apartment and desperately tried to close it. The problem was that, as always, she had far too many cute outfits for just one suitcase.

After staring at the piles of clothes for a moment, she finally decided to she had to make a supreme sacrifice. She had to take at least *one* out.

She narrowed her eyes as she considered what she could possibly live without. Finally, after some deliberation, she pulled out a scarf and tossed it on the couch.

Then she put her foot on top of the suitcase and tried, once again, to close it.

But even losing a scarf didn't help. Her clothes still bulged out the sides of the suitcase.

CeCe sat on top of it, hoping that the extra weight would force the suitcase closed long enough for her to snap the lock.

"Just got to—" she muttered, grunting at the effort.

It still wasn't working. Then she had an idea.

"Flynn!" she called out. "Are you still bored with your life?"

Her brother came into the room. "Yeah, why?" he asked.

"'Because I really, really need you to sit on my suitcase," she said, hoping that sounded exciting enough for him.

"I'm not *that* bored," he said with a slight sneer. Then he thought it over. "Wait, yes I am."

He climbed on top of the suitcase.

"Okay," CeCe said. "All right. Push! Keep pushing. Okay. Not go—oh! It's not working. What am I going to do?"

"Let's see. Maybe we can wave a magic wand over the suitcase to make it bigger," Flynn began sarcastically.

Then he pretended to have an even better idea. "Or—" He shouted the last few words—"*take some stuff out!*"

CeCe took a step back, as if Flynn's yelling was actually pushing her away. *For a little kid*, she thought, *he can be really forceful*.

Then she noticed that his shoulders had slumped. He seemed to have lost all of his energy.

"Wow, even yelling at you has lost its luster," Flynn said, depressed.

Then he took another look at what CeCe had packed.

"Wait a minute, you're going to clean up a swamp and you're bringing dresses and high heels?" he asked.

"Hey!" CeCe exclaimed. "You got to look good to *do* good!"

He eyed her suspiciously. "Why do I think you're up to something?"

"Don't be silly," CeCe said as casually as she could. "Now, hypothetically, if you were the judge of a reality dance show, would you prefer the gold lamé or the black ruffles?" She held up two dresses for his inspection.

He rolled his eyes. "And bored *again*."

♪ ♪ ♪

A short time later, the cast of *Shake It Up, Chicago* was on the bus and on the road.

Tinka got out of her seat and approached Gary, who was standing in the aisle. Even though they were only on a bus and there was no chance of an audience seeing them, Tinka had taken special care to look good. She had curled her long blond hair and put a sparkly silver ribbon through it.

"Gary, what time will we get to Alabama?" she asked.

"Well, the whole trip should take about seventeen hours," Gary said. "What time is it now?"

The words had barely left his mouth when he realized what a bad idea it was to ask that question. Sure enough, Tinka's eyes lit up and a smile flashed across her face in a way that Gary had already seen far too many times on this trip.

"It's a quarter past time to sing!" she announced brightly.

Gunther jumped up from his seat with a big smile, holding a ukulele. He, too, had dressed up by wearing a glittery vest over his shirt.

"That's the fifth time I've fallen for that," Gary groaned.

"Here's one everyone knows," Gunther said cheerfully. He began to sing. "Who stole the *goofinhookin* from the *goofinhookin* jar?"

Tinka gasped, as if she had just realized the answer to this musical question. "*Gary* stole the *goofinhookin* from the *goofinhookin* jar!" she sang in response.

"No, Gary didn't!" Gary snapped.

"Okay, then," Gunther sighed. He started back down the aisle, followed by his sister.

Then he spotted CeCe and Rocky sitting together. Rocky was wearing headphones and an eye mask and trying to sleep, but CeCe was still awake.

Gunther's eyes lit up. "CeCe stole the *goofinhookin* from the *goofinhookin* jar!" he sang.

But CeCe was in no mood for a sing-along, especially when the words were as goofy as the ones in Gunther's *goofinhookin* song.

"Gunther, if you don't stop singing, that jar is getting *stuffed* in your *goofinhookin*," she snarled.

Tinka and Gunther frowned at her. Then, imitating CeCe's annoyed tone, they muttered to each other. They did stop singing, though, and stomped away to the back of the bus. And that, as far as CeCe was concerned, spelled victory.

Gary stood in the aisle to make an announcement. "Okay, everybody, ten-minute bathroom break," he said as the bus pulled into a rest stop. "Go in pairs and stay together."

"Rocky?" CeCe nudged her friend, who was

napping in the seat beside her, eye mask firmly in place. "Rocky? Ro–"

Frustrated by the lack of response, CeCe lifted Rocky's eye mask and said even louder, "Rocky?"

"What?" Rocky looked around, blinking. "Are we in Alabama yet?"

"Um, no, bathroom break," CeCe said. "Come with me."

"I don't want to go to the bathroom with you," Rocky said. "I want to sleep!" She adjusted her neck pillow and tried to get back to her nap.

But just at that moment, Gunther's voice came drifting from the back of the bus. "Rocky stole the *goofinhookin* from the *goofinhookin* jar. . . ."

"Who, me?" Tinka chimed in.

"Yes, you!" Gunther sang back.

"Couldn't be!" trilled Tinka.

"Then *who*?" Gunther warbled.

"Oh!" Tinka and Gunther said together. They each pursed their lips and placed a finger on their chin. They looked, Rocky thought, insane!

Rocky rolled her eyes. "On second thought, my *goofinhookin* is a little full," she said. "Let's go." She would rather forfeit her nap than listen to any more singing!

Grinning, CeCe followed her off the bus. It was time to put her plan in action!

# CHAPTER 4

**BACK IN CHICAGO,** Uncle Frank was faced with a tough decision. He stood in the middle of his pizza parlor and looked at Ty, who was wearing a Crusty's employee T-shirt. Ty was also holding a large yellow sign in the shape of an arrow and a pair of enormous sunglasses with bright green frames.

"Okay, I got one job and two of you," Uncle Frank said to Ty. "So whoever gets more customers to come in with their coupons gets it."

"All right," Ty said, putting on the sunglasses. "Come on out, Deuce! You're not the only one that looks like an idiot!"

Deuce slowly entered the room, looking sheepish. He was wearing red shorts over a tight red unitard. He was also wearing a pizza box–complete with a pizza–as a mask! He looked completely ridiculous.

Ty couldn't help himself. He snorted with laughter. "I stand corrected," he said. "You *are* the only one who looks like an idiot."

Deuce glared at his uncle. "Okay, how come *he* gets to look cool and *I'm* in this costume that's doing no favors for my self-esteem?" he demanded.

"Yeah, yeah, stop complaining and go put on that pizza face mask," Uncle Frank said, trying not to laugh.

Deuce's glare deepened. "I'm wearing it and

you know it," he said through gritted teeth.

Uncle Frank and Ty burst out laughing.

"I'm teasing!" his uncle chuckled. He put an arm around Deuce's shoulders. "I tease because I love."

Deuce had heard this before. He still wasn't buying it. He just shook his head. "Could you love me a little less?" he asked.

His uncle wasn't listening. "Okay, boys, show me what you're going to do to attract customers," he said. "Deuce, you're up first."

"Okay." Deuce cleared his throat and held his arms out as he got ready to make his pitch. "Coupons!" he droned. "Get your pizza coupons!"

Uncle Frank shook his head in disbelief. This was worse than he could have imagined.

"Wow," he said. "I'll never get that jingle out of my head now." He turned away to Ty and said, "Okay, what do you got?"

This was Ty's big chance, and he was determined to make the most of it. He stepped forward and launched into an original rap about Crusty's pizza.

Uncle Frank was impressed. When Ty finished, Uncle Frank cheered. "Hey! Wow! Whoo! That was—"

He suddenly caught sight of Deuce, who looked dismayed. He tried to look serious.

"Well, looks like it's going to be a tight race," Uncle Frank said. Then he glanced at Ty and grinned. "Right, Ty? Wink-wink."

"Yeah," said Ty, grinning back at him. He felt a little sorry for Deuce, but come on! The kid didn't have any moves—and he really wanted this job!

♪ ♪ ♪

"Good morning, sleepyhead!" CeCe said enthusiastically. She looked over at her best friend.

Rocky blinked sleepily, then looked around. She was very confused. "Morning? Wait, shouldn't we have been in Alabama hours ago? Why are we still on the bus?"

CeCe bit her lip. "There, um, there was a lot of traffic," she said nervously.

Rocky sat up straighter. "In the middle of the night?" she asked. She looked around the bus. The other passengers were all strangers. *"Where is everybody else from the show?"* she demanded.

An older couple sat across the aisle from them. Hearing the panic in Rocky's voice, they glanced at each other, then gave Rocky a questioning look.

CeCe knew the truth was about to come out, but she still tried to delay the moment when Rocky would realize how she had been fooled. "What are you talking about? They're right here," she said, pointing to the older couple. "Hey, Gunther and Tinka."

"Wait," Rocky said, forcing a smile. "You tricked me into getting onto the wrong bus last night when I was half asleep, and now we're on our way to Los Angeles to audition for a reality show, aren't we?"

CeCe looked both guilty and gleeful. "Well, I feel like you want me to say no, but–"

"I cannot *believe* you did this!" Rocky shouted. She crossed her arms and stared straight ahead. She was furious!

"Okay, you're a little miffed, but you'll be thanking me when we're crowned the winners of *Really? You Call That Dancing*?" CeCe said, trying to assure her.

Rocky gave her a withering look. "Really? You call that an excuse?"

CeCe threw her hands in the air. "Oh, come on, just go with it," she said. "One day you'll look back on this and laugh."

As if on cue, they both heard a soft chuckle.

"There you go!" CeCe said happily. "See? I was right."

"I'm not laughing," Rocky snapped.

Again, there was the sound of a giggle.

CeCe looked mystified. "Well, I'm not laughing, either," she said.

This time, the laugh was a little louder. The two girls looked at each other in confusion.

"And if you're not laughing and I'm not laughing, *who's* laughing?" Rocky asked.

CeCe and Rocky both looked up at the luggage rack. Without speaking, they both jumped up and hauled down CeCe's red suitcase. When they opened it, they found the source of the laughter—and more trouble than they had counted on!

Flynn popped out of the suitcase, grinning.

"Right," Rocky said flatly. Could this day get any worse?

"Flynn!" CeCe yelled. "What do you think you're doing?"

Flynn glanced from his sister to Rocky. His eyes sparkled with mischief as he repeated the advice that Rocky had given him.

"Having an adventure!" he cheered.

# CHAPTER 5

**"YOU ARE EIGHT YEARS** old." CeCe said sternly. "You can't just pick up and take a trip on your own!"

Flynn rolled his eyes. "Yeah, apparently you have to be thirteen to do it," he said. "By the way, kudos on the L.A. switcheroo. I didn't see that coming."

"Mom must be freaking out," CeCe said.

"Relax. As far as she knows, I'm on a Coyote

Ranger camping trip," Flynn told her.

"You know, for a police officer, your mom doesn't do much investigating," said Rocky with a slight laugh.

Flynn chuckled. "Good one, Rocky," he said. "You're a lot funnier when we're on adventures together."

But Rocky did not share the joke. "This is not an adventure," she snapped. "I've been hijacked and you're a stowaway!"

"That happens to be the pilot for the new *Pirates* movie, which I don't need to remind everyone is—" Flynn gave a dramatic flourish of his hand—"an adventure!"

CeCe smiled. "I love those movies," she said happily.

"Me, too!" agreed Rocky enthusiastically. For the moment, she forgot that she was mad at her best friend. "Hey, maybe when we're in L.A. we can go on one of those movie-studio tours, and–" She stopped in mid-sentence. "What am I saying? We are *way* too young to be traveling across the country by ourselves. We can get in a lot of trouble!"

The older couple sitting across the aisle glared at her. "Shh!"

"Oh, chill out, Gunther and Tinka," Rocky said crankily. She plopped back into her seat. CeCe and Flynn squeezed in next to her.

CeCe decided it was time to offer Rocky a little friendly encouragement. "We'll be fine as long as we all stay together," she said. "Lighten up. Have a few laughs."

"I can jump out of the suitcase again," offered Flynn. "That was pretty funny, huh?"

CeCe gasped, her eyes wide. "I just realized something."

Rocky laughed slightly. Finally, CeCe was realizing what a mistake she had made–and it was about time!

"That you owe me a huge apology?" she suggested.

CeCe rolled her eyes at that. "No," she said. "If Flynn was in my suitcase, then"—she glared at her brother and added in a threatening voice—"where are all my clothes?"

Flynn stared back at her, unafraid. In fact, he curved his finger so that his hand looked like a hook and said, in his best pirate voice, "Arr! There wasn't enough room for me and the clothes, so I made them walk the plank. Arr!"

CeCe groaned. This couldn't be happening! Not after she spent so much time picking out her cutest outfits—and so much energy getting the suitcase to shut.

"Don't worry, CeCe, you can borrow some of my clothes," said Rocky. Even though she was mad at CeCe, she couldn't let her friend wear the same clothes the whole trip. Rocky felt a little glow of satisfaction about how generous and forgiving she was being. A lot of friends, she thought, would hold a grudge. A lot of friends would say, "I have a whole suitcase full of outfits, but I'm not going to lend you any of them." A lot of friends—

And that's when it dawned on her.

"Wait," she said slowly. "You forgot my suitcase on the other bus, didn't you?"

CeCe looked guilty.

With a scowl, Rocky curved her hand into a claw. "Arr!"

♪ ♪ ♪

Meanwhile, the rest of the *Shake It Up, Chicago* cast had arrived in Alabama and had started work on their charity project. A banner that read SHAKE IT UP CARES had been hung near the bus.

Gunther and Tinka were stretched out on lounge chairs in front of the sign. They were dressed in matching outfits that they thought were appropriate for cleaning up the environment—overalls, orange shirts, and zebra-patterned baseball caps. However, they weren't actually collecting any trash. Instead, there they were on the lounge chairs, surrounded by full garbage bags. They each held small, portable fans, which they pointed at their faces to keep them cool. All in all, Gunther and Tinka were very comfortable, which made it that much easier to smile kindly at the other cast members as they wearily walked up and dropped another pile of garbage at their feet.

"It's so peaceful and quiet," said Gunther. "So unlike the city. No bad smells, no loud, irritating noises."

Tinka nodded in agreement. "Hmm, that reminds me," she said. "Where are Rocky and CeCe?"

"I haven't seen them since we got off the bus." Just then, Gunther spotted the show's host. "Gary!" he yelled.

Gary walked over. He was wearing high black rubber boots suitable for wading through a swamp and carrying a trash bag.

"Where are the annoying ones?" Tinka asked.

Gunther raised his handheld fan and pressed a button. It turned out that the fan also squirted water—in this case, right into Gary's face!

"I'm looking at them," Gary said, giving Tinka and Gunther a hard stare. When this didn't seem to faze them, he went on. "You mean CeCe and Rocky? Rocky wasn't feeling well at the last bus stop. Fortunately, CeCe's aunt happens to work at the ticket booth and was planning a hot-air balloon trip to Chicago anyway." He chuckled, then walked away.

"What a *highly* unlikely coincidence," said Tinka. She turned to Gunther. "Are you thinking what I'm thinking?"

"That we should have gone for the silver

sparkly hip boots instead of the gold sparkly ones?" asked Gunther.

"No. Obviously the girls snuck away," Tinka said. "If we can catch them, we can get them in trouble *and* get them kicked off *Shake It Up, Chicago,* which means more airtime for us."

"How are we going to sneak away from the trip?" asked Gunther.

"Gary! Gunther isn't feeling well und our uncle's submarine just pulled up!" Tinka called out.

Gunther shook his head. "Oh, come on," he said, "he's never going to–"

"Safe trip!" Gary called back.

# CHAPTER 6

BACK AT CRUSTY'S, the contest between Ty and Deuce was heating up. Uncle Frank sat behind a table with two piles of coupons. The pile on his right had been brought in by Deuce. It was six inches high. The one on his left had been brought in by Ty. It was two inches high—at the most.

"Hey, hey, hey!" Uncle Frank exclaimed, holding a hand over each of the piles to measure them. "Look at that!"

Deuce grinned, looking confident. He had worked really hard and the results were there for all to see. He had beaten Ty, not just by a little bit, but by a lot! He couldn't wait to see his friend's face when Deuce was handed the job.

"You guys brought in the same exact number of new customers," Uncle Frank continued. "It's a tie."

Deuce's smile disappeared.

"Hey, I didn't think I did that well," said Ty, surprised and pleased.

"You didn't!" Deuce snapped. "My pile's *way* bigger."

But his Uncle Frank ignored him. He took half the coupons from Deuce's pile and put them with Ty's coupons, making both piles even.

"Ah! Yep," he said. "Looks like we're going to need a tiebreaker." He walked to the middle of the room, where two large objects sat under a black cloth.

"Now, half of my business is in delivery," Uncle Frank said. "The key—" He pulled the cloth aside, revealing two exercise bikes—"is getting there fast."

Grinning, he handed each boy a pizza box. "Okay, now whatever you do, don't lose the pie," he warned them.

"Okay," Ty and Deuce said at once.

Holding the boxes, they each climbed on an exercise bike and started pedaling.

At first, this seemed easy. Deuce was even beginning to feel confident again.

Then Uncle Frank added a twist to the contest.

"However, there are some obstacles along the way," he said. "Deuce, look out for that truck!" He blew an air horn right in Deuce's ear.

Startled, Deuce almost dropped his box.

Uncle Frank laughed. "It's a rabid dog, Deuce, a rabid dog!" he cried, barking.

Deuce screwed up his face, trying to

concentrate, but it was hard to focus with his uncle screaming at him like a maniac.

"It's a pack of rabid dogs!" Uncle Frank yelled, barking even more wildly. "With long fangs!" He pinched Deuce with a pair of tongs.

Deuce yelped. This was some contest!

Uncle Frank laughed and ran over to a table. He picked up a bowl of oranges and started throwing them at his nephew.

"Whoa! Look out, Deuce!" He tossed an orange at Deuce's head. Deuce ducked and barely avoided getting hit. "Look out!"

Deuce gave him a dirty look. "Let me guess. I'm behind a fruit truck?"

"Yes, that's right," Uncle Frank said, chuckling. He put the bowl of oranges down and picked up another bowl filled with tomatoes, carrots, and celery. "And it just crashed into a vegetable stand!" He threw the vegetables on top of Deuce.

He ducked to avoid the tossed salad that was

raining down around his head and gasped, "Wait a minute. What about Ty? Doesn't he get any obstacles?"

"Yeah, of course he does," said Uncle Frank. "Uh, slow down, red light . . ."

Obediently, Ty pedaled slower.

"Green light," Uncle Frank said, beaming as Ty started pedaling faster. "Great job!" He gave Ty a high five—causing Ty to drop his pizza box.

"Ooh, here, let me get that for you," said Uncle Frank as he reached down to pick up the box.

"Are you kidding me?" Deuce said, outraged. This contest was turning out to be totally unfair!

♪ ♪ ♪

Hundreds of miles away, the bus that CeCe, Rocky, and Flynn were on pulled into a bus station in Pepe, Texas. The station was an old, weathered wood building that looked like it had been built a hundred years ago. Still, they were glad to see anything besides the endless highway they had been on for hours.

"Ah!" sighed CeCe as they got off the bus and went inside. "Feels good to get off that bus, huh?"

Rocky didn't answer. She strode across the floor, heading for the ladies' room.

"So, we got about ten minutes. What do you want to do?" asked CeCe, following close behind. "Stretch your legs?"

Again, Rocky didn't say anything, but her answer was quite clear as she slammed the door of the women's restroom in CeCe's face.

"Or continue ignoring me like you have been for the past couple of hours," CeCe added, staring at the closed door.

"Finally, a bathroom break!" Flynn exclaimed, heading for the men's room.

Quickly, CeCe jumped in front of the men's room door. "Na-uh-uh," she said warningly. "Not by yourself. You can come into the ladies' room with me."

Flynn gave her a disgusted look. He was much too old to have someone chaperone him during a bathroom break—and he was certainly too old to go in the ladies' room!

"You know what?" he said. "I can hold it—till we're back in Chicago, if necessary."

As he walked away, he spotted a glass display box in the middle of the bus station. "Hey, CeCe, check it out," he said, reading the words on the box. "PEPE, TEXAS, HOME OF THE WORLD'S SMALLEST BALL OF TWINE."

CeCe sighed impatiently. "Flynn, what do I care about a stupid—" Then she caught sight of the ball of twine. "Wow, that *is* tiny."

Flynn turned back to the situation that had developed between his sister and her best friend. "So, what are you going to do about Rocky? She's really mad at you."

"Oh, please! Rocky's my best friend in the whole world. She can never stay mad at me," CeCe said confidently. Just then, Rocky came out of the ladies' room. "Right, Rock?"

"Uh-huh," Rocky said. But as she walked past CeCe, she gave her a bump with her hip that knocked CeCe off her feet and into a rocking chair.

"Thank you, Rocky, I *will* take a seat," CeCe said, trying to stay cheerful.

After all, Rocky was her best friend! She couldn't stay mad forever!

Could she?

# CHAPTER 7

**THE PIZZA DELIVERY** challenge had finally come to an end. Deuce and Ty had been allowed to get off their exercise bikes and were now sitting at a table, waiting to hear who had won.

Once again, Deuce was feeling good about his chances. He knew he had done well in spite of Uncle Frank's air horn honking and dog barking and produce-throwing antics. Still, he crossed his fingers for luck—just to be on the safe side.

Then Uncle Frank held up a clipboard with their scores on it and said gleefully, "I can't believe we have another tie!"

Ty gave a little chuckle as Deuce's mouth dropped open.

"A tie?" Deuce asked incredulously.

"Mm-hmm," Uncle Frank nodded.

"A *tie?*" Deuce's voice got louder.

"Yeah," Uncle Frank said.

"How was that a tie?" Deuce demanded. "The only rule was 'don't drop the pizza.' And in case you didn't notice, he dropped the pizza! *Four* times!"

"Wow," said Ty. "I had no idea you were so competitive."

He stood up and put his arm around Uncle Frank in a friendly manner. "Can you believe this guy, Uncle Frank?"

Deuce's eyes widened in anger. "He's not your uncle, he's *my* uncle!" he sputtered, jumping to his feet. He turned to Uncle Frank. "And I don't understand why you're always mean and picking on me."

"Hey, hey, hey, that's no way to talk to your boss!" his uncle replied.

"M-my, my *what*?" Deuce stammered. His eyes lit up with hope. "Y-you mean you're giving me the job?"

"Of course I am," said Uncle Frank. "I was always going to give you the job. You're my nephew, you half-baked calzone!"

Ty's jaw dropped. "Wait a sec, that's nepotism!" he cried.

"If, uh, nepotism means that I'm afraid of his mother, then yes, it's nepotism," admitted Uncle Frank.

"If you were going to give him the job all along, why'd you put me through all that?" Ty demanded.

Uncle Frank shrugged. "You're right," he said.

"You're *both* hired." He picked up a bucket. "Go ahead and get started," he said, taking a toilet brush out of the bucket and tossing it to Ty. "It's a big job."

Ty looked at the toilet brush in disgust. "On second thought," he said, handing it to Deuce, "he won fair and square."

"Okay, Deuce, get to work," said Uncle Frank. "And take off that stupid pizza mask."

Deuce scowled at him. "I took it off and you know it!" he said through gritted teeth.

Uncle Frank and Ty couldn't help it—they burst out laughing. That joke just never got old!

♪ ♪ ♪

In Texas, CeCe and Rocky were sitting on a bench inside the bus station, waiting for the announcement that it was time to get back on board. Rocky's arms were folded across her chest as she stared grimly into the distance. Next to her, CeCe was giving Rocky a sad look. She had a feeling she had made a big mistake.

"Rocky," she sighed. "Are you still mad at me?"

"Not at all," Rocky said angrily. She looked down at her nails.

"Oh, good," CeCe said, relieved.

"Hey, do you have any change?" Rocky asked suddenly.

"Yeah, sure," said CeCe. She dug in her pocket, then handed Rocky some coins. "Here you go." As she handed them over to her friend, Rocky threw them back in her face!

CeCe blinked. "Feel better?"

"No, but I will as soon as I call my mom on the pay phone and tell her everything!" Rocky snapped. She grabbed the coins and stomped over to the phone.

"What?" CeCe gasped. "Why would you do that?"

"Because I'm not getting bars on my cell," Rocky said crossly. Surely even CeCe could figure out how hard it was to get cell-phone reception in the middle of nowhere!

"No. I meant, why would you tell your mom?" CeCe asked, getting up and walking over to her friend.

"Because this trip was supposed to be about helping people, and you made it all about you!" Rocky yelled. "Calling my mom is the right thing to do. And you're not going to convince me that it's not."

CeCe nodded, admitting defeat. "You're right. I had no right to drag you into this," she said sheepishly. "It was a stupid idea."

"Not working," Rocky said, tapping the phone buttons in annoyance.

"Fine," said CeCe. She sighed. "I'm really sorry, Rocky. I guess I spend so much time dreaming of us being amazing dancers who bring joy to people and I thought maybe going on *Really? You Call That Dancing?* would speed things up. I guess I'm just in too big of a rush to make it all happen, but I wasn't being selfish. I did this for *us*."

She paused, hoping that her heartfelt confession would convince Rocky to forgive her.

Rocky glared at the phone. "Still not working," she complained.

"No, I meant it," CeCe insisted, her eyes wide. "I wasn't trying to talk you out of calling your mom."

Rocky turned to face her. For the first time, she realized that CeCe had misunderstood. "No, the *phone*!" she explained. "It's not working!" She hung up and walked back to the bench. CeCe joined her there.

"Next bus stop, we'll call your mom and go home," CeCe said.

Rocky gave her friend a small smile. "Thank

you," she said. They both slumped on the bench, their elbows propped on their knees and their heads hanging down.

But as they sat there, tired and sad, the air suddenly filled with music. It had a lively beat and, almost without realizing it, CeCe and Rocky's feet started tapping in unison. Before they knew it, their feet started moving from side to side. After all the months of rehearsing and dancing together on *Shake It Up, Chicago*, the two girls had a natural sense of how to move together. Without even trying, they found that their feet were going back and forth in unison.

They both jumped to their feet at the same moment and began dancing, each girl's moves matching the other's in perfect rhythm.

Rocky couldn't help smiling, even though she knew, somewhere deep inside, that she was still mad at CeCe. But just now, it didn't matter. Now they were dancing together, like old times, and it was as much fun as always.

As the music ended, Rocky and CeCe each threw an arm up in a flourish.

Then Rocky turned to CeCe, her eyes sparkling with excitement. "We could *so* get on that show," she said.

She stopped, realizing what she had just said. CeCe held her breath, hoping that her dreams were about to come true.

"Okay, fine," Rocky finally said.

"Yes! Yes! Yes!" CeCe jumped up and down in excitement.

"Our moms are going to kill us anyway," said Rocky. "They might as well wait until we get back home from Los Angeles."

"Really?" CeCe asked. This was almost too good to be true! Not only was Rocky not mad at her anymore, but she had actually agreed to go to L.A.!

"Yeah," said Rocky. "With any luck, we'll win,

For a special *Shake It Up, Chicago* performance, CeCe wore fierce glow-in-the-dark makeup.

The *Shake It Up, Chicago* dancers performed a final run-through and nailed it!

Tinka was excited to volunteer for *Shake It Up Cares* in Alabama.

CeCe wants Rocky to skip *Shake It Up Cares* and go to L.A. with her for an audition for a new reality dance show.

The glow-in-the-dark performers hoped to *glow* the audience's minds!

Rocky, CeCe, Flynn, Ty, and Deuce met for the opening of Crusty's, a new pizza place owned by Deuce's uncle.

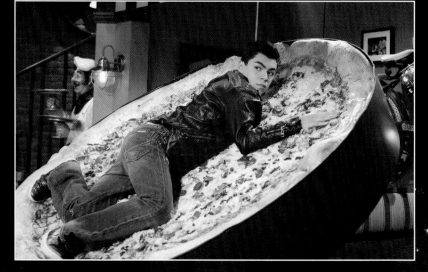

Deuce proved that Crusty's really did have the world's deepest deep-dish pizza!

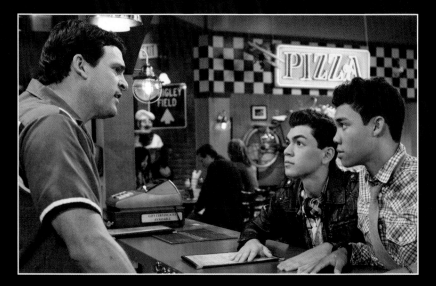

There was a job opening at Crusty's. Deuce and Ty both wanted it.

"I've only got one job and two of you. Whoever gets more customers to come in gets the job," Frank said.

Ty came up with an awesome rap to attract more customers. Frank was impressed.

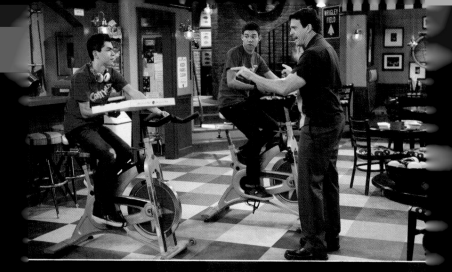

Frank gave the guys another task—to prove their pizza delivery skills. "Whatever you do, don't lose the pie!" he explained.

"Look out for that truck!" Frank yelled as he blew an air horn in Deuce's ear.

Gunther and Tinka hoped to get the girls kicked off *Shake It Up, Chicago* by telling CeCe's mom about the girls' plan.

Even though they didn't make it to the audition in L.A., CeCe and Rocky got to perform at an air show.

Rocky and CeCe were told they'd be dancing on the
wing of a plane—while it was flying!

CeCe was nervous. "Look I know we didn't plan this,
but let's go for it!" Rocky said.

there'll be a tour afterward, and we'll never have to go home."

Flynn strolled over, grinning. "I had a feeling you guys would work it out and we'd wind up going to L.A.," he said, putting on a pair of sunglasses. He turned to give a thumbs-up to the weathered cowboy sitting behind the ticket counter. "Hey, Narvel, thanks for letting me use your boom box!" he called out.

Narvel nodded and tipped his cowboy hat to Flynn.

Then the sound of a bus engine starting up echoed through the room.

Rocky ran to the door and looked outside. Her face fell as she turned to face CeCe and Rocky with the bad news.

"I think we just missed the bus," Rocky said. "What now?"

"Uh, um, no, no, no, it's fine, it's fine," said CeCe. "We'll just, uh, hang out here and then catch the next bus to L.A., which is in . . ." She squinted at the bus schedule on the wall, "three days."

Rocky sank down on the bench. This trip was turning out to be a huge mistake. What were they going to do now?

# CHAPTER 8

**"I DON'T UNDERSTAND** why there wouldn't be another bus for three days," Rocky complained.

"If you were a bus driver, would you be in a rush to come back here?" Flynn asked.

"So that's it?" asked Rocky, sitting down again. "We're just stuck here?"

"No, Rocky, don't worry," CeCe said. "We can still get to L.A. in plenty of time to audition."

Rocky shook her head in exasperation. "How

can we still go to L.A.? The next bus is in three days. It takes two days to get to L.A. and four days to get home. How many days is that, CeCe?"

"Uh . . ." CeCe wrinkled her forehead, then said, "Hey! I don't do math unless I'm in class."

Flynn rolled his eyes. "And even then it's fifty-fifty." He caught CeCe's puzzled look and added kindly, "Which means only half the time."

"Look, if we're not home by the end of the week, we're going to get in huge trouble," said Rocky. She went to the ticket counter and picked up a bus schedule.

"All right," she said, scanning the schedule. "Okay, there's a bus to Chicago tomorrow morning, and we have to be on it."

CeCe sighed.

"I'm really sorry, CeCe," added Rocky.

"No!" CeCe cried. They had come so far—she wouldn't let their dreams be shattered just yet.

"No, we can't just give up that easy! We're in Texas. We can discover oil, make a billion dollars, buy an airplane, fly to L.A., and still be home on time!"

Rocky gave her a look. "CeCe."

CeCe's shoulders slumped. "All right, fine, it's over," she admitted.

Both girls sat back down on the bench.

"Whoa, whoa, whoa!" Flynn exclaimed. "That's it? We're just going to hop on a bus and go home?"

"We don't have any choice, Flynn," CeCe said. She was doing her best to sound reasonable and mature, even though she secretly agreed with Flynn—it was horrible that they had to abandon all their hopes and dreams just because of something called reality!

"Great," Flynn grumbled. "You totally wrecked my adventure." He stomped over to the vending machine. He knew that getting a snack wasn't going to make him feel any better. On the other hand, it couldn't make him feel any worse. And he was hungry, as usual!

But the whole world seemed to be against Flynn. He dropped his coins in the slot, pressed a button and—nothing happened.

"Oh, come on!" he yelled. Annoyed, he kicked the machine.

Still nothing. "This is *not* my day," he muttered.

He was so intent on getting his candy that he didn't notice a girl about his age standing nearby. She wore jeans, a checked shirt, and cowboy boots. Two blond braids peeked out from under her red cowboy hat.

After watching Flynn's battle with the vending machine for a few more moments, she strolled over and gave the machine a kick. Instantly, a candy bar dropped down. She picked it up and handed it to Flynn.

Flynn took it, surprised and pretty impressed.

"Thanks, stranger," he said. "I'm Flynn, from Chicago."

She nodded. "Name's Bo," she said, introducing herself.

"Isn't that a boy's name?" Flynn asked.

Bo raised one eyebrow. "Ever heard of Little Bo Peep?"

Flynn shrugged. "My bad," he said. "So, Bo, what do you guys do around here for fun?"

"Nothing much," she said. "Mainly we like to do this." She pulled out a water gun and sprayed him, grinning.

"Stop that!" Flynn sputtered.

"Sorry," she said. "I was just messing with you. Hey, look up there!"

She pointed at the ceiling. Flynn looked up. As soon as he did, she squirted him again, then giggled. "Aw, city boy is so scared, he wet his pants," she said in a jeering voice.

"No, I didn't!" Flynn argued.

"Yeah, you did," Bo insisted. She squirted him one more time before dashing out the door.

"That's right, you *better* run!" Flynn called after her. "Flynn Jones is coming for you! Just as soon as I go to the bathroom and sit on the hand dryer." He stomped off to the men's room, fuming. This adventure was not turning out at all the way he had planned!

# CHAPTER 9

THE *SHAKE IT UP, CHICAGO* cast trip to Alabama had ended. Tinka and Gunther were back in Chicago, intent on proving what they suspected was true—that CeCe and Rocky had made an excuse to run away earlier, breaking their promise to help clean up the swamp.

The first step, they had decided, was to break into CeCe's apartment and see what evidence they could find. Of course, they had to bring a bit of sparkle and glam to this operation—after all, that was the way Tinka and Gunther rolled!

They crouched on the fire escape and carefully opened the window of CeCe's apartment, dressed, of course, in matching black burglar outfits. And of course, their black T-shirts were covered with sequins. Tinka had even added an extra touch of fashion with a black sequined hoodie. Trust it to them to make breaking into someone's apartment an opportunity to make a fashion statement!

As they eased through the window, Tinka said, "Now we will find out—did Dopey and Dopier come home or go somewhere else?"

Gunther nodded. "Once we have the evidence, we will bust them and they will be off *Shake It Up, Chicago* forever," he said enthusiastically.

They both burst into laughter. Then, as if reading each other's minds, they both stopped at the same moment.

Gunther crossed the room in a low crouch, followed by Tinka.

"Are you *sure* there's no one home?" Tinka asked in a low voice.

"Yes, I checked," Gunther said. "Flynn is on a camping trip, and the mother works eight to six every day this week."

"Yeah," Tinka said, relieved.

"Unless she takes a personal day," a new voice said.

Tinka and Gunther whirled around to see Georgia, CeCe's mother, walk into the room, eating an apple.

"Correct," Gunther said. "Unless she takes a—" Suddenly, it dawned on him who he was talking to. "Uh-oh."

♪ ♪ ♪

Uncle Frank walked into the pizza parlor, where Deuce was wiping off a table. He stammered,

"Deuce, ah, my friend, uh, Remo is, um, he's getting paroled and you know I promised to speak at his hearing and . . ."

He stopped and threw his hands in the air. "Uh, who am I kidding? You're family. He's breaking out and someone's got to go pick him up. You keep an eye on the place, all right?"

"No problem, Uncle Frank!" Deuce said cheerfully. He was so grateful to be a Crusty's employee that he would do anything his uncle asked!

♪♪♪

In Pepe, Texas, dozens of people were crowded in a large room in the town hall. A large sign on one wall said, AIR SHOW KICK-OFF DANCE. Along another wall, a long buffet table filled with food had been set up. A group of people were filling their plates.

CeCe was ready to join the crowd, but Rocky held back.

"Um, CeCe, we can't just waltz into this party," she said.

"Oh, we'll blend in," CeCe said airily. "Just follow my lead."

As she pulled her friend into the room, Rocky looked around. She wasn't sure that "blending in" would be as easy as CeCe thought. Everyone else was dressed in country-western clothes: blue jeans, cowboy hats, and boots. She, on the other hand, was wearing a brightly colored mini-dress over her jeans, while CeCe was wearing plaid pants and a vibrant T-shirt.

CeCe, however, had no doubts, as usual. She walked up to a man who was piling his plate with food.

"So, you think the rain will hurt the crops this year?" she asked chattily.

The man gave CeCe a puzzled look. Rocky

rolled her eyes. Surely even CeCe should know that crops needed rain to grow! Talk about not blending in!

As the man walked away, CeCe tried to save the situation. "Me neither," she called after him.

CeCe looked at Rocky and shrugged. "Come on," she said, walking across the room to find other people to make friends with.

As Rocky followed her, Flynn approached the buffet table, his eyes shining. "Hello, beautiful," he said to a platter of baby-back ribs. "You're a little bony, but I like that in a rib." He glanced down the table and saw bowls of potato salad, pots of chili, and platters of enchiladas. "Whoa! Texas *is* an adventure–a *culinary* adventure!"

As he began filling his plate, he spotted a red cowboy hat sitting on the end of the table. It looked familiar.

"Hey, that looks like my old friend Bo's hat," he said. He smiled to himself as the beginnings of a beautiful plan for revenge popped into his head. But he had to work fast—Bo was standing a few yards away with her mother.

A few seconds later, Bo's mother walked right past the table, headed for the door. She didn't even glance over to see Flynn crouched behind the table, hiding.

"I'll be right there, Ma," Bo called after her. "I just got to get my hat." She hurried over to the table, picked up the hat, and put it on her head. Instantly, gravy poured down over her blond braids.

She gasped.

Flynn jumped up, laughing. "You want some biscuits to sop up that gravy?" he asked.

Bo glared at him through dripping gravy. "That's *so* not cool," she snapped.

"Relax," Flynn said. "You got me, I got you, now we're even." He held out his hand for a friendly fist bump, but Bo just ignored him.

"You messed with my hat," she hissed. "Around here, a man *never* messes with another man's hat. You'll be sorry!"

As she ran after her mother, she cried, "Ma! My hat's ruined!"

# CHAPTER 10

**ACROSS THE ROOM,** CeCe and Rocky were sitting at a table, eating. They had blissful expressions on their faces, as well as a great deal of barbecue sauce.

"Mmm," CeCe murmured through an extra-large bite. One thing she had to say for Texas—the people here *really* knew how to make barbecue! It was the best she had ever had! Her eyes were half-closed as she enjoyed the tangy, mouth-watering taste–

"Cute boys, cute boys!" Rocky muttered under her breath, interrupting CeCe's meal. She tilted her head toward two boys about their own age who were leaning against the wall watching them. One had slightly long dark hair and the other had a nice smile. They both wore large cowboy hats.

"Say something!" CeCe whispered urgently.

Rocky frantically searched for a cool and casual way to strike up a conversation. Finally, she remembered what CeCe had said about blending in. *That's it!* she thought. *I'll try to sound like I belong in Texas!*

"Howdy, guys," she said. "I'm Rocky, and this is my partner, CeCe."

"Hmm," CeCe murmured in greeting.

The boy with long hair smiled. "I'm Ethan," he said, tipping his hat to her. He pointed to the other boy. "And this is Aaron."

"They like us," CeCe said under her breath to Rocky, giggling a little. "They can't stop staring."

Rocky took a good look at her friend. "That's because you have food all over your face."

CeCe looked back at her. "You, too," she said.

Rocky's eyes widened in horror. "Oh, no!"

"Oh, yes," CeCe said.

Fortunately, this didn't seem to matter to Ethan and Aaron.

"Y'all want to dance?" Ethan asked.

Rocky brightened. "You bet your sweet tea we do." She grinned. This day was turning out to be better than expected!

♪ ♪ ♪

It was a good thing for CeCe that she didn't know her mother had found out about her and Rocky running away from the *Shake It Up, Chicago* bus trip. It would have totally spoiled the fun of dancing with two cute Texas boys if she could have seen her mother pacing angrily around the living room as Tinka and Gunther sat quietly on the couch.

"Who does she think she is, getting off that bus?" CeCe's mom fumed as she held her cell phone to her ear. She listened for a moment, then grimaced. "Oh, great," she said. "Voice mail." She spoke into the phone in a deep, scary voice, "Call me."

Then she hung up and turned to Tinka and Gunther. "Now it's time to use that tracking device I put on her phone." A few moments later, she frowned. "Texas?" She looked puzzled. "She's in Texas? What is she doing in *Peepee*, Texas?"

Gunther walked over to look at the phone screen himself. When he saw the town's name, he said snottily, "I believe it's pronounced 'pay-pay'."

"Yeah? Well, I'm going after her, and when she sees me, she's going to *pay-pay* her pants," CeCe's mom said. She couldn't believe that her daughter was so far away. She had to get to Texas, and fast!

# CHAPTER 11

**THE AIR SHOW KICK-OFF** dance at the town hall was in full swing. Dancers turned, stomped, and swung around in two lines as onlookers clapped along to the music. At first, CeCe and Rocky hung back, watching in amazement as the dancers on the floor performed a line dance in perfect unison. They had never seen dancing like this—but it looked like a lot of fun!

After a few moments, they ran onto the

dance floor, ready to join in. They began dancing with Aaron and Ethan, kicking up their heels and stomping their feet as if they'd been dancing like this for years.

Then CeCe had an idea. She rushed over to the table where they had been sitting, grabbed a CD, and took it to the DJ.

"Hey, can you play this?" she asked. "Thank you!" She smiled and ran back to the line of dancers. When her music started playing, it wasn't country-western. Instead, it was an upbeat modern song that was one of CeCe's favorites.

Rocky and CeCe grinned at each other. This was more like it! They started busting their own moves, the ones they had practiced in rehearsal after rehearsal at the *Shake It Up, Chicago* studio.

The other people on the dance floor looked at one another. What CeCe and Rocky were doing wasn't line dancing—not by a long shot—but it looked amazing! One by one, they began following CeCe and Rocky's lead. Before long, everyone was dancing to this hip new song.

When the song ended, everyone cheered. CeCe and Rocky smiled at each other, a little breathless. A few moments later, a man in a gray suit and cowboy hat walked over to them.

"Excuse me, girls," he said. "I'm Mayor Bartlett, and can I just say I've *never* seen such fine dancing."

CeCe curtsied to him and said, "You can say that all day long, Your Highness."

Rocky had to resist the temptation to roll her eyes. Didn't CeCe know that you only called royalty–like kings and queens and princes–Your Highness? Or that town mayors were addressed as 'Your Honor'? She made a mental note to nag CeCe a bit more about doing her history and civics homework, then hissed, "CeCe, he's a mayor. It's 'Your *Honor*.'"

CeCe gave a light laugh. "I'm so sorry,"

she said. "It's my honor, Your Highness."

Rocky tried not to groan. Fortunately, the mayor just laughed.

Rocky smiled and held out her hand. "I'm Rocky, and this is CeCe."

"Well, it's my pleasure," the mayor said, beaming. "You two are very professional."

"Oh, thank you," Rocky said. "We dance on a show called *Shake It Up, Chicago.*"

The mayor frowned. "Don't believe I've ever heard of it."

CeCe felt a little sorry for Mayor Bartlett. Imagine not having heard of Chicago! "Oh, um, it's a pretty big city in Illinois," she explained.

"Wow, she can dance *and* she's funny," the mayor said, grinning. "Listen, girls, tomorrow's our big air show. We're expecting over a thousand people, and our two dancers dropped out. We're having a heck of a time replacing them. Is there any way that you—"

"We'd love to—" CeCe interrupted.

"But we can't," Rocky finished, shooting CeCe a warning look. Had she forgotten that they had to get home as soon as possible?

"But—" CeCe started to protest.

"No," Rocky said firmly.

"But—" CeCe tried again.

"No!" Rocky's voice was even more stern.

"But—" CeCe couldn't give up. They were being offered a chance to perform! It was what they both lived for. How could Rocky say no?

Easily, it seemed. "No," Rocky said again.

"But—" CeCe was pleading now.

It didn't change Rocky's mind.

"No!" she snapped in the kind of "and-that's-final" voice that mothers often use.

"Okay, fine," CeCe said and pulled Rocky aside. It was time to have a word in private, away from the honorable mayor.

"See, I just thought that since we never

got to audition for that reality show, dancing in front of all these people would make up for it," CeCe said.

"You're not the only one who didn't get what they wanted this week," Rocky pointed out. "I wanted to help people. That didn't happen either. Deal with it." She walked back to the mayor. "Look, we have to be on a bus first thing in the morning."

Mayor Bartlett looked disappointed. "Oh, well, looks like we're going to have to refund the ticket sales. There goes our school arts program," he said sadly.

"Wait," Rocky said. "If the school doesn't have an arts program, then students get bored, drop out, crime rates rise, stores close, jobs disappear, families move away, and before you know it, Pepe is flushed away, like it never existed in the first place." She stopped for a moment, imagining this bleak future. Then she broke into a big smile.

"I'm going to save a town!" she declared, smiling at her best friend.

CeCe jumped up and down in glee. "And *I'm* going to dance in front of a thousand people," she squealed.

"And *I'm* going to get re-elected," Mayor Bartlett said with a big grin as he walked away. It was a win-win situation for everyone!

The girls were still smiling when Flynn came up, a frown on his face.

"Uh, guys?" he said. "I'm not sure about this."

"Not now, Flynn," CeCe said impatiently.

"But you don't know what you're–" Flynn began.

"Flynn!" Rocky interrupted him. "This is the first time CeCe and I have been on the same page this whole trip."

"Exactly," CeCe agreed. "And we're dancing

in that show tomorrow. Come on, Rocky, let's go work out our choreography."

Flynn raised his eyebrows. "Or you can just *wing* it," he suggested.

But CeCe and Rocky were too excited to pay attention to what he had just said. They had dance moves to practice!

# CHAPTER 12

**THE NEXT MORNING,** Rocky, CeCe, and Flynn went to the field where the air show was to take place. Another delicious-looking buffet had been set up. Flynn's eyes lit up as he looked over the food. People in Texas really knew how to eat!

"I can't believe it," he said. "A deep-fried pig in a blanket with bacon-maple dipping sauce? I love Texas!" But he didn't have time to pick one up, let alone eat it, because just then, Bo sauntered over.

"Howdy there, Flynn," she said. Her manner seemed friendly enough, but Flynn knew better than to trust it.

"Hey, Bo," he said cautiously.

"Look, Flynn," Bo said. "I've been thinking about what you said before, and I'd really like it if we could be friends."

Flynn was puzzled, but he didn't want to keep this feud going. He and Bo weren't the Hatfields and McCoys, after all! Even more important, if they kept fighting, he wouldn't get a chance to eat those delicious deep-fried appetizers. "Wow, it takes a big man to say that," he said.

Bo grinned. "Shake on it, then?" She held out her hand. She was wearing a bright green rubber glove.

Flynn took it, then a look of disgust crossed his face. "You got something kind of warm and squishy in your hand," he said. "Did your mom make fudge?"

"No, Bessie did," Bo replied, giving Flynn a wink.

A horrible thought filled Flynn's mind, but he tried to push it away. "Is Bessie your sister?" he asked, hoping for the best.

"No, she's my cow," Bo said, finally breaking into laughter. "You just got cow-pied! Cowgirl, two; city boy, one."

As she ran off, Flynn glared after her. "Oh, this is *not* over yet," he muttered But he had to admit, Bo got him good this time!

Behind him, CeCe and Rocky emerged from the building where they had changed into the costumes for their dance performance. From their white cowboy hats to their blue unitards decorated with red stripes, red stars, and white fringe, they were a star-spangled vision.

"There they are," the mayor called out. "There are our stars!"

Rocky was pleased, but she believed in at least sounding humble. "Oh, I wouldn't say we're stars," she said modestly.

"Rocky, the man's a mayor," CeCe said. "This is his town, go with the flow."

"Tell you what, this is the best turnout we've ever had," the mayor noted with satisfaction. "Why, I haven't seen folks this excited since we cut the ribbon for the new speed bump."

"So, uh, where's the stage?" asked CeCe. She looked around. All she could see was an open field, a crowd of people, and a red plane that looked like the ones people flew back in the early twentieth century.

"Right over there," the mayor said, pointing.

CeCe peered in that direction. "Oh, um, I,

I can't see the stage; that rickety old plane is in the way,'" she said.

Mayor Bartlett grinned. "That rickety old plane *is* the stage," he explained. "You'll be dancing on the wing."

Rocky's jaw dropped. Surely she had just misheard him! Surely the mayor couldn't have just said the completely crazy thing that she thought he said!

"Why would we do that?" she asked, really hoping that there was some kind of mistake.

"Because it's an air show," the mayor said patiently.

CeCe's face turned pale. "You, you mean the plane will be flying?" she stammered.

"You betcha," the mayor replied.

CeCe and Rocky exchanged looks of panic.

"In the air?" Rocky said, just to be clear.

"You betcha," the mayor repeated.

CeCe felt as if she were going to faint.

"So, when you said the other dancers dropped out . . ."

For the first time, the mayor looked sad. "You betcha," he said.

CeCe and Rocky looked at each other, terrified. What had they gotten themselves into now? And how would they ever get themselves out of it?

# CHAPTER 13

AT CRUSTY'S, DEUCE was taking his responsibilities seriously. After all, his uncle had left him in charge! He had talked Ty into pitching in, hoping that he could keep everything running smoothly until Uncle Frank came back.

As Ty wiped down the counter, Deuce said, "Hey, man, thanks for helping me out."

Ty looked up. "I'm not helping you," he reminded Deuce. "You're paying me."

"Fine," Deuce sighed. "Just put this on." He held out a pink hairnet.

Ty gave it one look, then shook his head and laughed. "Yeah, *not* going to happen."

"You *have* to wear a hairnet!" Deuce insisted.

Ty's shoulders slumped. He should have known. "Health-code regulation?" he asked.

Deuce rolled his eyes. "No, it's for my own amusement," he said sarcastically.

Ty wasn't happy, but he knew he had to put the hairnet on. After all, it wasn't safe for people to work with food and not wear one. He was smart enough to understand that. He just wondered whether Deuce was smart enough—and mature enough—to not make fun of him.

As Ty pulled the pink hairnet over his head, his question was answered. Deuce pointed at him and snickered loudly.

Ty glared at him, and Deuce quickly pulled out a piece of paper with a list on it.

"Okay," he said. "So we have to set the tables, fill the cheese shakers, and make dough."

"I'll get the silverware," Ty said, heading for the kitchen.

"Okay," Deuce said. Left on his own, he began putting together the ingredients for the pizza dough.

First, he peeked into the large pot sitting on the stove.

"All right, uh, water's in," he said. He turned to the list and read out loud. "'Then add water.' Okay." The directions called for flour next. He poured some in from a bag without measuring it.

"Okay, that seems enough." He read from the list. "Now, yeast. Okay." But before he could add the yeast, the phone rang. "Oh, I got it!" he called out. As he ran to the phone, Ty came back from the kitchen.

"Okay, it's dough time," he said, rubbing his hands. He took a look at what Deuce had already done. "Uh, flour's in. Water's in. Next is yeast."

He grabbed the box of yeast, poured some into the bowl and examined the results. "That doesn't look like enough." He added even more. "There."

"Hey, Ty, your cell phone's ringing," said Deuce from across the room.

As Ty left to answer his phone, Deuce walked back to the bowl.

"All right, now where was I?" he said to himself. "Oh, right, the yeast." He shook more yeast into the pot, then examined the results.

"That doesn't look like nearly enough," he muttered to himself.

As Deuce started adding more yeast, the phone on the counter rang. He picked it up.

"Hello?" he said. "Oh, hey, Uncle Frank. How's your friend Remo?" As he listened to angry, squawking noises coming from the phone, he kept pouring more yeast into the pot. "Yes, it's fine," Deuce said impatiently in answer to his uncle's question. "You don't have to check up on me. I'm not an idiot."

With that, he tossed the empty box of yeast aside and opened a new one. He threw some more yeast in and then, finally satisfied, he left to go into the kitchen.

The pot of water, flour, and yeast started to bubble in a very scary way. . . .

# CHAPTER 14

**TWO CHAIRS WERE BOLTED** to the wing of the plane that was about to take off at the air show. As Rocky and CeCe strapped themselves into the chairs, CeCe said nervously, "Uh, Rocky, why are we going through with this?"

Rocky was pale but determined. "The arts program, remember?" she said. "Plus, it's karma. We *did* drop out of *Shake It Up Cares.*"

"And *now* we have to drop out of the sky to

make up for it?" CeCe asked, her voice edged with hysteria.

"Don't you worry about a thing, darling," Mayor Bartlett said. "We got us a great pilot. Wave to the dancers, Stan!"

The pilot turned around in his seat and gave them a cheerful wave. Rocky tried not to look horrified; CeCe did her best to ignore the sudden cold lump in the pit of her stomach. The pilot looked as if he were at least a hundred years old!

"You have *got* to be kidding me!" CeCe shrieked.

"Oh, nobody knows this plane better than Stan," the mayor reassured her. "He flew it. In World War One."

The lump in CeCe's stomach got bigger. "World War *One*," she hissed to Rocky. "How old does that make him?"

"Just be thankful you're not good at math," she said, trying to remain calm. "*Or* history."

CeCe moaned. "Rocky, I don't think I can go through with this."

"No, sure you can," Rocky said. "Okay, we just won't look down and we'll pretend like we're onstage and it'll be over before you know it."

"That's what I'm afraid of," CeCe said.

"Look, I know we didn't plan this, but here we are, so let's just go for it," Rocky suggested. "Come on, life is about finding some excitement, having an adventure."

This did not make CeCe feel any better. "Please, that's just the advice you gave Flynn," she reminded Rocky.

"No," Rocky replied. "That's what I learned from being friends with you."

For the first time since they found out they were going to dance on a plane that was flying through the air, piloted by someone who was a century old, CeCe smiled. She held out her hand to Rocky. Rocky took it. They both sighed, happy to know that they were still friends, come what may. They looked at each other bravely.

Then the plane's engine started. It was about to take off!

Suddenly, Rocky realized exactly what they were doing.

"On second thought, this is crazy!" she cried. "Let's get out of here!"

"*Thank* you!" CeCe said with relief. As they began unbuckling the straps, they heard a voice over the engine roar.

"Back out?" the voice said. "I don't think so."

CeCe turned sharply and saw Flynn pop up from the backseat of the plane.

"Flynn!" she cried. "What are you doing?"

He grinned and thrust his arm into the air. "Having an adventure!" he yelled.

Rocky shook her head ruefully. "Last time I ever give that kid advice," she said.

"Okay, there is nothing in the world that

anyone can say or do that is going to keep us on this plane," CeCe said, tugging at the strap again.

"Hey, CeCe?" Rocky was looking across the field at the area where cars were parked. "Isn't that your mom's car coming toward us?"

CeCe's eyes widened with panic. "Floor it, Grandpa!" she yelled at the pilot. "Go, go, go!"

The two girls pulled goggles over their eyes as the pilot took off. Whether they liked it or not, they were about to be airborne!

# CHAPTER 15

**DEUCE AND TY HAD ALL** the glasses and silverware organized and were getting ready to set the tables in the pizzeria.

"I think my uncle is going to be pretty impressed with the job we did," said Deuce.

He was so satisfied with himself that he did not hear the ominous bubbling sound coming from the pot on the stove.

"Hey, how come I'm the only one wearing

a hairnet?" Ty asked. He was so annoyed at looking like a pink-hairnetted idiot that he did not see the dough rising out of the pot.

"Hey, I don't make the rules, I just enforce them," Deuce replied. "Stop making a big deal. You can hardly tell you're wearing it." Grinning, he held up his cell phone and took a picture of Ty.

"Man, how much pepperoni did you eat?" Ty asked. "I can hear your stomach growling."

"Um, that's not my stomach," Deuce said.

They turned finally—and saw a huge, monster blob of dough overflowing the counter! The dough slid messily to the floor. Deuce and Ty screamed. Now what?

♪ ♪ ♪

Rocky and CeCe were screaming, too—although in their case it was because they could look down and see the ground speeding by hundreds of feet below them!

"How cool is this?" Flynn asked. He was thoroughly enjoying his plane ride.

CeCe and Rocky gave him dirty looks. Couldn't Flynn understand how much danger they were in? Couldn't he understand that this wasn't fun at all?

Just then, the pilot's head dropped to one side. He began snoring loudly.

"Uh-oh," Flynn commented.

"Whoa, whoa, whoa, what's going on?" asked Rocky.

"Nothing," Flynn said quickly. "Our pilot just fell asleep. Or he died." He leaned forward to get a better look at Stan. "Wait, no, his chest is moving," Flynn reported. "He's just sleeping."

The plane tilted to one side. CeCe and Rocky screamed again. "Flynn, do something!" CeCe shouted.

Flynn reached down and grabbed the controls.

Within seconds, the plane had righted itself.

"Okay," CeCe said with relief.

"We're safe, we're safe!" Rocky shouted.

"Who says video games are a waste of time?" Flynn yelled over the engine's roar. He made a mental note to tell his mother how all that time learning to use a joystick had saved all of their lives. She would probably be very happy to hear that—right before she killed them all for ending up in Texas!

♪ ♪ ♪

Back in Chicago, Deuce was trying to beat the pizza dough back with a broom. It was a fight to the finish—and the dough was winning.

"Ty! Ty!" he yelled. "Where are you, man? I need your help!"

Gasping for breath, Ty poked his head out from the mass of pizza dough, which had flowed over him. "Help!" he cried.

Deuce looked at him, shocked. "Dude, where's your hairnet?"

"Really?" Ty asked, annoyed. "*That's* what you're worried about? Because if you haven't noticed, I'm in the middle of a blob!"

Just then, Deuce heard the phone ring. "Where's the phone?" he asked worriedly.

"In here," Ty said, nodding at the dough. Deuce pushed his hand into the dough and felt around. He managed to find the phone and pull it out of the gooey, sticky mess.

"Crusty's Pizza," he said. "Delivery? Sure, hang on a sec, let me get a pen."

He looked at Ty. "Can I get a pen?"

Ty rolled his eyes, reached into the dough, pulled out a pen, and handed it to Deuce.

"Thanks." Deuce took the pen, then said into the phone, "Okay, so that's one large meat-eater . . ."

"Aren't you forgetting something?" Ty asked pointedly.

"Oh, yeah, thanks, man," Deuce said. "Anything to drink with that?" he asked the customer on the phone.

Ty stared at him, amazed that his friend could take a pizza order while he was trapped inside a mound of man-eating dough! Deuce is really taking this job seriously, he thought. *Way* too seriously.

♪ ♪ ♪

It seemed to CeCe that their plane ride would never end—or that it would end in a terrible, fiery crash. But if that was their fate, CeCe was determined to make amends with her best friend before it happened.

"Rocky?" CeCe said.

Rocky turned to look at her. "Yeah?"

"I'm so sorry I switched buses on us," CeCe said. "We should have just gone to Alabama with *Shake It Up Cares.* You were right."

"Thank you," Rocky replied. Then she gave her friend a fearful look. "Oh, no! The only reason you're apologizing is because you think we're about to die!"

Flynn interrupted this serious conversation with a concern of his own.

"Hey, start dancing before we run out of fuel," he shouted. "Less yippy-yap, more tippy-tap."

Rocky nodded. Flynn had a point, she thought.

"Here goes!" she shouted.

# CHAPTER 16

**AS THE MUSIC STARTED** playing, Rocky and CeCe began to dance. True, they were still strapped into their chairs, but they tapped their toes, swayed to the music, and waved their arms to the beat.

Before they knew it, they were even smiling and having fun. After all, what could be better than dancing for a big crowd of people—even if the crowd was hundreds of feet below them on the ground!

And indeed, everyone in the audience was watching every move they made as the plane soared through the air. Everyone, that is, except CeCe's mother, who was frowning at her cell phone. What she was looking at on the screen didn't make sense.

"CeCe? CeCe, where are you? Where—" She shook her cell phone. "I don't get it, it says she's right here. No, wait—"

She stared at the phone screen, then pointed in the opposite direction. "Now she's over there." She looked at Gunther and Tinka, puzzled. "How does she move so fast?"

Tinka wasn't listening. She was staring at the sky angrily. She turned to Gunther. "Why don't *you* come up with snazzy ideas like dancing on an airplane wing?" she complained.

"Because not only do I have fashion sense,

I also have *common* sense," he pointed out.

Up in the sky, CeCe and Rocky were smiling as they finished their dance routine.

When the music ended, the crowd on the ground cheered loudly. CeCe and Rocky grabbed hands and laughed.

"Oh, my gosh!" CeCe exclaimed. "Look at us! We did it!"

"I know," Rocky said. "And it was actually kind of fun."

But down on the ground, CeCe's mother was getting more and more confused.

"I don't get it," she said again. "I think this stupid thing is broken because it says she's right here."

"Actually, she's right *there*," said Tinka, pointing at the sky.

CeCe's mom looked up and gasped. What was her daughter doing sitting on the wing of a plane? And what was Flynn doing leaning out of the plane and holding what looked like a water balloon?

Flynn squinted at the ground. Even from high in the sky, he could see Bo's red cowboy hat. She was standing right there next to two people who looked a lot like Gunther and Tinka. He frowned. What would those two be doing in Texas. . . ?

Then he shook his head. This is *not* the time to get distracted, he told himself. This is the time for *revenge*.

"Okay, Bo. You had this coming!" he yelled. "Here comes some Bessie lemonade!" He heaved the balloon into the air. It rocketed toward Earth, then burst on the ground—right in front of Bo, Gunther and Tinka.

"Aah!" Bo yelled.

"I stand corrected," Gunther gasped. "It *is* Peepee, Texas."

Once the air show was officially over, CeCe's

mother made sure that everyone came back to the car with her. She even counted heads—twice—to make sure that no one had managed to sneak off when she wasn't looking. Then she looked sternly at her daughter.

"For starters, you're grounded forever, I'm shaving your head, and I'm giving away all your clothes," she said. "Except for the purple velour sweatshirt and track pants your grandma gave you for Christmas."

Gunther chuckled at the thought of CeCe wearing purple velour. Even better, the image of her wearing a tracksuit! "That's a good start," he said to CeCe's mom. "Now tell them they're off *Shake It Up, Chicago*."

CeCe's mother glared at him. "Yeah, I would," she said, "except, keeping her on the show is *your* punishment. You should have called me as soon as you realized they were missing!"

Flynn didn't want to call any attention to

himself at this particularly tense moment, but he couldn't help it. He laughed as he saw Gunther's face fall.

His mother pretended to laugh with him, then said, "Yeah, keep laughing, Flynn," she warned.

Flynn opened his eyes wide, hoping to look innocent. "I told you, Mommy, it's not my fault. CeCe *made* me go with her!"

His mother gave him a warning look as CeCe glared at him.

Flynn hesitated, but he knew he didn't have a chance of getting away with his story. "All right, it was worth a shot," he said, shrugging.

Rocky stepped forward. If everyone else was getting into trouble, it was only fair that she take some of the blame.

"I'm so sorry, Ms. Jones," she said earnestly. "I've already written an essay about how this whole thing—"

"Oh, can it, Rocky," CeCe's mom interrupted. "I'm still ratting you out to your mom."

Wincing, Rocky sat down next to CeCe, trying not to think about how much trouble she'd be in when she got home.

"Okay, now what highway does that map say we should take?" CeCe's mother asked in a businesslike way.

CeCe opened the map she was holding. "Highway sixty toward Amarillo," she said promptly.

"Okay, let's go." CeCe's mother led the way toward the car, trailed by Flynn, Gunther, and Tinka.

Rocky and CeCe stayed behind. Even in the midst of worrying about what her mother was going to say to her about this escapade, she felt there was something wrong about what CeCe had just said.

"Wait, are you sure about those directions?"

Rocky asked, taking the map from CeCe. "Because highway sixty will take us to—"

She stopped in mid-sentence as she realized what CeCe was planning. Rocky couldn't believe it! After all they'd been through, CeCe still wouldn't give up!

"We're going to L.A., aren't we?" she said with a stern look.

CeCe grinned. "Well, she's already shaving my head. What else do I have to lose?"

They walked after the others arm-in-arm, and Rocky started laughing.

True, she was probably going to be in a lot of trouble when she got home, but in the meantime, she was still with her best friend—and about to go on yet another adventure!